# GOD IS IN FULL CONTROL:

## TIME IS IN REVERSE PART II

BY JENNIFER DIANNE THOMAS

# COPYRIGHTS

# DISCLAIMER

*Only God Alone is responsible for any and all results including content as well as conclusions for any and all materials through Jennifer DiAnne Thomas, A.K.A. Mu'men 'Elleyyeen...*

# TABLE OF CONTENTS

*WELCOME TO PART II.*

*ENJOY YOUR JOURNEY*

# "THE UNGODLY CHIROPRACTOR IS FORCED TO PAY..."

A young woman went to the chiropractor for professional services… In return, he rubbed his private on her left foot…during the visit… The young woman had already expressed to him earlier that she was having a serious breakdown in her life… The male chiropractor then used this information…and took advantage of her… Later on, he overcharged her for services of $250.00 per visit…and her insurance company refused to pay… That's when he tried to get his money, but only God alone took over his business and allowed him to get sued for another incident…as evidence against the chiropractor, who groped her while performing chiropractic services… Furthermore, in God alone plan, the chiropractor has a special place in the pits of prison hell…as the final abode.

It was 7:40p.m. on July 03, 2011.

# "THE 20TH CENTURY SELF-CENTERED EGYPTIAN STORY…AS WELL AS MANY OTHERS…"

I'm a fish without water,

I can't live without you… I respect you…

If you get me to your country…we will work and save lots of money.

We need to make a family…but I'm broke…

I can't afford to give you anything for marriage.

Can you get me there…but you need to come to me first for marriage. I need a marriage visa from your country…then I can help you…

Otherwise it won't work…

God will help us…

I know that things will work…

My friends are marrying other women from other countries also… "The women are not smart here…"

I need you…

All of a sudden, the tables turn…

I hate you,

I don't trust you…

You didn't give me enough money…

You make me look bad in front of my family…

"I need a white woman…because here in Egypt, she is known to submit to mankind."

No Salaamu Alaaykum

Hey, Egyptian, guy…

Women are not supposed to pay for their own dowry…

You lied and used Islam to gain my attention… This is an outrage; you're a "Hislam?"

No worries, I will trap you here in my country on the blackball list in minutes…and you will never be able to leave my country…

You signed the contract…

I don't speak your language…I thought it was Islam…

Islam means submission to God alone and not man…

It's called never using Islam or any religion to manipulate someone for anything…especially a

marriage visa.

Or you will be a fish without "heaven, and from only God alone."

Welcome to reality; family values are misused everywhere…

It was 9:20p.m. on July 03, 2011.

# *ENERGY HAS A WAY OF CHANGING, SO BE CAREFUL WHO YOU TRUST...*

This life on earth is all an illusion.

The devil's turf is fabrication and trying to make an illusion seem as though it's reality... In the end, after falling into the devil's trap...everything becomes unbalanced and broken down to nothing, zip, zero, zilch, and in pure negative form, from the signature of hell.

Everything from God alone 3.14 PI. The system is never fabricated... In the end, no matter what, God balances everything.

It is 10:19a.m., on June 10, 2011.

This battle started before we were born...we will understand everything in heaven...but now we are soldiers for God alone, and we must keep fighting and

win together in full unity as one...

# *Journey to Freedom: Unveiling the Heavenly Keys of Peace and Love*

On May 31, 2011, from 6:19p.m. to 7:19p.m., God alone taught me the value of having the keys of heaven… On my way to the river, dogs started barking and running… immediately. God alone allowed me to use what God put inside of me, to be free… Yes, the key to heavenly freedom… As I blew and whispered Allahu Akbar…, God is great…with peace and love…I continued as I waved my hand towards the oversized dogs, and they stopped abruptly, and in the silence of peace, and God said that they heard me… As their owners looked in awe and as if they'd never seen their dogs lie down and set down their paws, and stop barking… Of course I said, all praises be to God alone… As I kept walking in aw…and further down the street, I saw the geese, in peace, and God told me that they are free on earth, to have love and tranquility… Then, I sat down on the bench directly in front of the river. I couldn't help but look up, and then I saw the angels hook up, with collaborations, of many smiles, from heaven… Again, I said all praises be to God alone…and I love you all… However, after a while, God said to me that it was time to go… As I looked over to the window, I heard the laughter of children, running in water and playing…

God said, keep walking, and I did… On my way out of the park, I looked up and saw a dark man, with demons all around, and inside of this man… Then, directly ahead of

him was a posted sign that said vehicles prohibited, and he
ignored the rule, and he continued on and opened the gate,
and I said, Oh my God, what is this… God told me, when
you look at shit, you step in shit… You hold the key to

heaven and NOT hell… So I said, okay, thank you, as
the concern of my former thoughts fell…thank you, God,
alone, that I didn't earn the key of hell… …That's when I
used the dirt and grass for tissue…, to clean the dog poop,
off of the bottom of my gym shoe… …and on my way, I
saw a man with dreads… Why? I don't know; my locks are
clean, and I don't have dreads… God alone explained to
me that I'm not dreadful, so I cannot have dread.
Furthermore, while God alone continues to walk and talk
with me… The same guy with dreads, I noticed, who has a
huge stomach, and I smelt his poisons from a distance…
Then the guy stared at me while he was on his cellular
phone, and I thought, who is going to clean him… God told
me that he did it to himself.

Then God showed me the river of puddles…and I said
thank you, God, now I can clean my gym shoe… So I
did…and it was clean… Then God told me to walk further,
and I saw more homes near the City of Detroit Mayor's
mansion…

Then I thought about my experiences at The
Jeffersonian Apts. and said, I have to leave not only the east
side of Detroit, Michigan…, I need to cross the border…
Then God alone showed me a newborn baby bird that fell
from out of its nest, and it was on the ground trying to flap
its best, but the movement of its wings was to no avail…
This situation got the best of me, and God told me not to

touch it…because the mother's scent needs to know it… Again, I listened to God alone because it is God alone that got me here, and never will I disrespect God, who is the holder of our throne…and many will know… God said, again, you hold the keys of heaven, inside of you… So I asked God to help the baby bird while he flapped his wings, and I heard a man with two dogs coming while he held them on a string… I couldn't let them hurt and or kill the newborn baby bird… The baby bird couldn't help itself.

So I stood there and looked at both of the dogs in their eyes, and I blew, whispers of heaven, and they immediately stopped… The owner, of the dogs, tried to get his dogs to move, but they refused… I said wow; this is how to use the keys to heaven… I said, thank God, the man looked at me, and I told him; please go around a baby bird… He said yes, it fell out of its nest he will die, because the mother won't know him… I said I don't want the dogs to eat the baby bird… He said don't worry they won't…and they passed… However, one of the dogs turned around, with a wagging tail, as the other sat down…in aw… Then I turned around in amazement, and I said thank you God, what can I do now… God said, again you have the keys to heaven, so I said, and asked God alone to help the mother find the baby bird… So I looked up and saw a bird, that appeared to look for the newborn baby bird in its nest…and she flew the other way… So I continued to stay, with the newborn baby bird, who continued to flap its wings, and he still couldn't do anything… I thought about what God told me, again, you have the keys to heaven…

So I prayed to God alone, to take it…to freedom…
Then I looked down and saw the bird rest, and its wings
were not flapping anymore… God showed me that the
newborn baby bird is in peace, and this is how you use your
key…to heaven… As God told me to walk, and keep
going… I saw a home with the address with number 20 in
it…and as I looked for number 19, it was long gone…
…and I realized, that I work for only God alone throne, and
I was number 19, and now I'm number 20. …All praises be
to only God alone in Arabic… God alone informed me that
I needed the Quranic code number 19 to get to
freedom…and through my strong…faith in only God
alone… I am number 20, with the pleasure of the presence
of God alone key to heaven. God is love and thank you
God alone. That's when God alone explained to me, that
God has given me, the key to heaven, in God alone
heart…and there is only one key to everything… The key
to heaven is accepted everywhere, and because God alone
placed the spiritual key to heavenly freedom inside of me, I
can go anywhere…with God alone.

So I continued my walk, and my walk became a stroll, and oh, the oversized black dog, tipped toed over to the fence in silence, and wagged its tail, while the white dog sat down and froze in aw… That's when I knew, what God alone what's me to do… Share the knowledge of peaceful

freedom, and help them from the ground bearing chains…of spiritual war…and everything…

Every time God shows the time…is confirmation…you don't need to look at number 19...because God alone Angels are number 20. Number 19 is the end of the quadratic code, but yet the beginning of number…20.

The reflection of God staring into my eyes, my face…is the message…and I see the story…that God alone has me writing…

Thank you only God alone.

# *SACRIFICE*

On June 2, 2011, God sent me to the river at the Belle Isle Bridge… Where I ate lunch, saw seagulls, ducks, and fishermen… The first fisherman that caught my attention was and eleven year old, with his mom in her 60s and she was the instructor… Then there was an older man with him, and he looked at me and said, "I can tell that you're in peace…" I told him that God alone did this for me… So he went along, further into a deeper conversation, and he asked me, so how would you fish? I told the man, well, I would pray to God alone before I threw the fishing pole and or net out into the water…for food to eat…and if God wills, I will… That's when I said my goodbyes and the mother of the young boy said, come back again; we enjoyed your company… As I left, God sent me down

further down the walkway, and a man with his son were fishing by themselves… God told me that I wanted him…the young boy that turned out to be 23 yrs. old… He was peaceful, I felt his heart…and he had natural youth…with a pure heart…

Regardless of flaws, God will fix him through and through… He taught me how to fish again from long ago; I forgot I knew what to do… Then it dawned on me that I was fishing for this man and for his freedom… Of course, he gave me his rod and allowed me to fish, but I didn't catch one until 8:19p.m. I attempted to catch another one, and then this older guy came along…as he used God alone name in vain… I thought, and God alone said, this is hell material…no respect and the young boy said, this is my brother…and he is in his forty's but almost fifty, so I was told… I began to leave, but God showed me the young man's pure soul, and he got the best of me… God told me to stay, and the young man said, "I don't like to fish alone…and this fish is for someone who is hungry…and his dad will clean it at home…" So I gave them my fish…and I realized that the fish that God allowed me to catch…was a sacrifice… As I prayed to God alone to take its soul, I learned my lesson today of the price of sacrifice…

## *PROPHECIES...*

Living your life through God will come naturally, and
things will work naturally... The laws need to reflect... On
June 3, 2011, at 5:19a.m., I woke up from a horrifying
revelation that demons are praying on the weak because no
one will stand up for them, including children... No dad
around to fight for them... Trusting mothers without
common sense that only live through ignorance... Be
careful because your child may be God alone, Angel... and
you better not let anything happen to them... God has
already warned you in your visions... Their cry will be the
death of many... If someone holds evil, lives evil, preys
evil, prey is evil, causes evil, thinks evil, and does evil...
Then their destination will be the hell. The devil's followers
are satanic thinkers... Selfishness is a crime...

## *ROYALTY*

As I began to kneel down and pray, God said get up, you're royalty… Didn't I give you the key, the only key to my heavenly kingdom? I answered? God said, yes, you've earned it… No one else deserves it. Look at what you were willing to come through… While the world questions me… You came through many souls of thee with yes, yes, yes, yes, God; you don't have to make me… I want to do it… and God said, and this is why you have my key of royalty… Heaven is your home, and your freedom has gotten everything…including me… You have my attention through my heavenly extension… As I breathe through preventions of evil and cast out devils, I fear no evil… For God is with me, as my rod and shield have comforted me… Today, I finally realized that I'm royalty from only God alone. It's 12:19p.m. on June 3, 2011.

# *PACIFIERS*

Pastors become pacifiers, thinking that this will help the problem… While the lost children sit outside on the bench… Who is praying to God that they're sick of this… Fake people, fake prophets, thinking the world needs to stop it… With fingers popping, hip-hopping, like they're in a club, getting what… Drunk like a thug… Dipping in cars, sneaking out of service, listening to chains of musical disservice… How, how, how did this happen? How can we get to heaven…? As I look at the devil stepping through each one of them…

I have no more words, oh, I'm stuck…

Where is freedom?

Freedom ring, and I'm not talking about any telephone company… PICK UP…

Here are your pacifiers…because you've messed up… It's 12:27p.m., on June 3, 2011.

# WHICH DAY?

Now, this Sunday, it's not a fun day… Do you need to be fiddly dumb and pop your fingers through the bible, looking for the next freedom… How about a riddle to catch the next message so your feelings won't hate it… The truth of why are many of you so down and blue… No, I'm not finished, are you? No, you stop it, promise to God alone, who sits high on the throne… You got it? Now hang up the phone…finger popping.

## *YOU...*

Can't convince a demon… So leave them to burn to death… There will be no help… In the depth of flames, where there are many remains…

It is 1:19p.m., on June 3, 2011...

# A DEMON, BIRTHING A DEMON...

What is there to say?

Well, they know the direction to take… Down…

They surely can't go up…because heaven's doors are shut…

# DEAD WEIGHT

Holding up the day, with dissipating, rejection, regulating… Wait, no one can move without you…

Who are you, in control of it all?

Where is your world? Do you have one?

Then, create it.

Wait, that brain is from only God alone. Wait, everyone came from only God alone. Wait, that vision is from only God alone.

Wait, are you fed up and going to walk away strong?

Those legs are from only God alone.

Wait, now what?

Using my elevated energy from only God alone so that you can shine… Why, because you can't afford to look into God alone eyes…

You're nothing, so poof, be gone…

It's called leftovers…

Of what, exactly…?

It's 1:40p.m., on June 3, 2011, to see the light from only God alone.

GOD IS IN FULL CONTROL, and "we are not."

# *YOU BETTER NOT RAPE…YOU FREAKING RAPISTS…*

Babies crying for freedom, yelling, what is between them? A murder of spiritual souls and chains… This day God will break…break "yo ass…" with your own pains… You've passed the hell test… Is this real? Hell yeah… Can you feel the violations…from heavenly sacrifices and parties of evilness that you forced on people… on earth…? Now hell is your birth, kum fiya kum…be, and it is…isn't it…as it's in you…freaking demons… How does it feel to be ganged and raped in hell, man…? Shhhhh…get a good look at his face… Close up, they all look alike, but lol he can't win this fight… Hell beats itself… "Like this southern girl in racist times, and or with demonic minds, "yelled he beat me…" …because he was a strong black guy?" What? Are you calling God for help? God wasn't included in your life on earth, remember? You blocked it… with B.S. of evil sockets… Hell is for stupid people, with deep pockets… it is June 3, 2011, at 2:07p.m.

# *LINE OF SYMMETRY REFLECTIONS...*

Did you see him do it? The police officer says, " What? The brother of the victim says, "I don't need to see him do it. The evidence is right there..." The police officers said, "Right where?"

The brother of the victim says, in front of you… Remember? I photographed the pictures and emailed them to you… Wasn't it good enough? The officer says no…we will not continue this investigation… So the police officers left the house and went to get coffee down the street, and a man rode on his bike directly up to their police car window, on the left side… The man on the bike said to both of the police officers, "Give me your wallets…" The police officers responded, what? Here is my badge… The man laughed, here is my gun…and it's a machine gun with much power… So the police officers tried to get a good look at his face, but the gun barrel was so long that their visions were blocked…and instantly life flashed before their eyes, and when they saw ghosts in disguise… The ghosts said, no, I'm your guardian angel. I'm not a ghost… LOL, remember me? You just left the scene of a crime that was mine…

It is 2:19p.m., on June 3, 2011.

It's called "Fencing from Heaven," at 2:20p.m., on June 3, 2011.

GOD IS IN FULL CONTROL, "and we are not."

Did you think about this when you've intentionally sinned? Now you're sacred? Heavenly favored? Naw, NOT, of course not... hypocrites, are who God alone wants... the two twisted-headed dogs, of fakeness...and without heart, as well as pureness... You can't win, so sit down and listen, read, read, read, read... Now get on your hands and knees while you plead...guilty, guilty, guilty, guilty, and guilty to only God alone. Now, are you willing to follow only God alone...? Then be with only God alone and change yourselves, so that you can sit in heaven...in God alone kingdom. By far....many of you are not...accepted.

# IF YOU DON'T LIKE IT…READ IT AGAIN,

because God alone likes it… It's called intelligence…

# WHAT ABOUT ME?

LOL, got taken over me… Sent me here on this earth, in disguise…amongst many of you…. I can do no wrong… because I follow only God alone. Get the memo… I didn't want to be around many of you because of evilness, as it undresses my heavenly intelligence…with exchanging energy of evilness… God had to come and get me, and cleanse my soul, through it all, over and over, and over again…. Now I'm pure, no thanks to man…

It is 3:14p.m. in math; this is called, 3.14 PI, from only God alone.

# *GOD ALONE SENT ME HERE....*

A long time ago, as an example…of the truth and light…and every day, I had to fight through the wickedness of chains…and the devil knew my name… Everything changed, and I had to remain the same and prove my name meant PI. Not just any pie, but supernatural pi, from only God alone. For some people, I had to pray to God alone to prevent me from snapping their necks because of evilness added on to no intelligence… Even in high school, I had to fight blind, as I was at war with this 300lb girl who pretended to be my friend… I lost my mind, and God took over my intelligence… While 3 police precincts with backup…was called to arrest me… …But God said, no don't worry…about beating her…she is the devil's kid… While God invested power in me… I began beating, stomping, and punching through…to freedom until this day…no record remains, even the judge of the courthouse backed off…on this day…

It is 3:20p.m., on June 3, 2011.

…Now God alone gave me to hold, the key of heavenly freedom…that is within me, from only

God alone.

This is God alone book…

Relax, sit down, be quiet and take a look… A gander… God alone the book is especially for a crook…to stop the wicked ways…while he continues to prepare the price to pay… What did you say? The loss of heavenly forever, eternal freedom… Did I bite my tongue? Lol, it is 3:40p.m., on June 3, 2011. -14.3 for the thief… Double knock on this…

# *A message to only proven Heavenly angels and on Earth, that are waiting to make your next transitions...*

God alone loves only the pure heart and soul people… Heaven awaits you…believe me… Your positive spirit is what makes everything float…and your humbleness is not in vain… God alone knows your name… Your beautiful spirits are what is in aw… You are rare in many situations. I understand you and I fight for your freedom with you… To God alone is the glory… Don't worry; God alone will take all of the evilness away from you…and bring it to a complete head…and busts… While the oppressors will be oppressed by their own evilness... God alone is now with them… You were never a spare tire that they violated and used… Now, they will continue to be abused… In hell… let me tell you… Your place in God alone kingdom is so bright, that even God alone heavenly angels look like lights of gold…but never old… So imagine your welcoming committee…and your heavenly home… Just remember that God alone is the best, has the best, and keeps the best. …No evil people allowed… …because heaven is too proud. Take time to think, at least 3 minutes….

It is now 4:19p.m., on June 3, 2011.

It's called no dead weight… is in heaven.

The devil knows this is how we float with God alone and without negative energy…

28

From only God alone. At 4:20p.m.

Selfishness is a crime; it's where the demons hide… Don't turn your back, or else…

God will not help you…

Now it's time…for the next level…

What you put in life…you get it back in return…

Just make sure that it's…**God alone, the heavenly kingdom of 3.14 PI.**

# SELFISH PEOPLE CAN'T HAVE PI.

A woman became famous, and only God alone financially blessed her life… Furthermore, on this one particular day, a woman said, I'm so happy to see you…and she was an awesome cook… However, this woman never cooked for the woman that only God alone has financially blessed… One day, the woman that only God alone financially blesses said to her hi, I'm Deanne…can I eat with you? The woman responded, oh, I didn't cook anything…and Deanne said, oh, I smell wonderful aromas from your kitchen… The woman says that's for my ex-husband and his family… So the woman that only God alone financially blessed left her neighborhood…and she never came to see her ever again… However, that very same woman needed a blood transfusion, and the woman that only God alone had financially blessed matched her blood type…and she needed a blood donation within 19 days… The problem is the woman named Deanne was out of the country traveling to the land where only God alone sends the prophets to provide messengers for the entire world…for 20 days… On the 21st day, the woman that only God alone has financially blessed continuously one-liner…heard the news that the woman cook had passed away due to selfishness…and only God alone gave Deanne the entire explanation for the selfish woman's death. God alone said to Deanne, you bought expensive dinner for this woman…and treated her amicably…and yet she had never cooked you food from her soul, not even prepared a fruit bowl. In heaven, everyone shares…and to only God alone, everything has to return… It was 9:20a.m. on July 03, 2011.

A woman thought that she was connected, and God alone told her that she had to be corrected…because she was not in line and didn't think that she was getting a dime… So take that fake façade off of her face…because she is about to be replaced.

Now hell has her face, at the end of the day… I told you that God doesn't play.

Now, this is the center of attention…

# ANOTHER TOOK CREDIT

A woman yelled at her child, "I brought you into this world, and I'll take you out…the same way that you came in…" Instantly, this disrespectful woman shook the heavens… Then God alone took notice, and the angels became angry… The woman began having heart problems…and tried to dial 911, the emergency number… Then God whispered into the disrespectful woman's ear canals…now what are you going to do…? Pray to you only God alone, she said….

# MISBEHAVING CHILDREN...

Several children went to school one day and disrespected a substitute teacher… When the children got home and finished dinner… they instantly became tired…and fell asleep… God came with chastising…and whooped the children until they pleaded guilty and vowed never to misbehave in life ever again… The very next morning, each child went to school and begged the teacher for forgiveness, and every day since then, they kept the other children in line…and helped the teacher for all of her days at their school.

# A WOMAN RECEIVED HER BLESSINGS…

A woman has worked for only God alone, and sacrificed everything…in life in order to achieve these goals…and from only God alone… God alone blessed this woman with a riverfront mansion, as appreciation and with infinity blessings from heaven… From this point on, God alone gave her 55 BILLION dollars as spending money, from someone else's hand…as a congratulations and on her heavenly successfulness and from only God alone kingdom…for winning the fight for the heavens…in only God alone name, and with only God alone help.

It was 11:20a.m. on July 04, 2011.

# ONE MORNING, GOD ALONE…

One morning, God alone woke up a 3.14PI person and dressed her to the bone… Took her out on a night of town for the entire weekend that she will never forget, and a young man passed her path with his girlfriend, and he looked at her, and looked back at his girlfriend and smiled…as he kept walking…his girlfriend looked back at the young lady that only God alone dressed to impress…in golden light…of 3.14PI., peace… Everyone looked as she walked in respectful grace, and the children in the mall instantly put a smile on their faces…as she stopped and told them about only God alone. Everyone stopped to listen and to see their reflections upon her dress with mirrors…while others frowned, upside down…but to her, it showed a smile from only God alone on the throne.

It's called: never compare your man and or woman friend… It's 4:20p.m., on April 17, 2010.

# *I CAN HEAR WITHOUT A PASTOR…*

I can hear without a Pastor because he is too busy under his secretary's dress… When God alone called, I answered…peacefully and gracefully in humbleness… God said, "I have a message for my people… I want you to deliver it…tell my people to stay and praise only me …the one and only God alone, on the throne. I would tell the Pastor, but he is too busy sinning and preying on people…

It's called a minister called straight to hell in a handbasket full of firing coal…as the devil's best man.

It's 6:07p.m., on 07/05/2011.

# *A MAN LIKES THEM BOTH...*

Males and females…are welcome… Singing in the choir
are the devil's praises…

Aids, it doesn't matter… Being free is the victory… They
say, come as you are…

…but no one is labeled, by far…that's their fight…

If they've paid attention…no one would get by…and need
intervention… It's called; don't overlook lost souls…before
you end up as their prey…

## *Do Not Worry About Whom Comes Upstairs...*

But dad, I don't want my friends to see you with a man...
They all laugh at me...

Son, you eat,

You're clean...

You get money every day...

Stay out of grown folks' business...

The son prayed to God...

Please help me...My friends are laughing at me... What can I do...?

One day, his dad had to be rushed to the hospital...for uterine cancer...and the doctors told him that he couldn't have any kind of sex...including in multiple places within himself...because he was infected with other diseases...that they would not mention at this time...

Furthermore, a female nurse read his chart, and the domestic man saw that she was so beautiful...and from that moment...he never wanted to be near another man ever again...

He saw heaven in her eyes...as she prayed over his soul...and cleansed him thoroughly with healing hands...

While he and the woman talked…the man told the female
nurse that he was molested by his mother's boyfriend when
he was younger…and he never kissed a girl in his life…

The man's son walked into the room, and he was
happy…with his prayers being answered…

# *NURSERY...*

Leave him alone…the 2-year-old baby yelled…

I'M TELLING HIS MAMA…

The baby ran and got an adult and pointed at the demonic man…who tried to touch the baby on its private…

Instantly, a ton of people ran over and jumped him…until he was unconscious…

All of a sudden, the news was being displayed on the television…

The people noticed that this man was wanted…and the 2-year-old baby said, "He is

mean…and a very bad person…"

…While they were beating him…

The lights went out…and the demonic man was dead.

Later on…the 2-year-old baby was rewarded with honors…from the city's Mayor's office…with a baby's bottle in hand.

The Mayor was so outdone…that he gave the microphone to the child's mother…and she said, "My baby has been speaking full complete sentences at 6 months."

The baby tapped its mother's leg and said, Mommy, I want to speak…" Hi, he was a bad man…

Thank God alone, he's gone…

Mommy, can I have my bottle back?

Yes, love…

God is good all of the time…

It is 7:20p.m., on July 05, 2011.

A message from God alone to the one who deserves their
needs fulfilled… I will give you lots of money very soon…
Don't worry.

It is 7:22p.m., on July 05, 2011.

Thank you. Only God alone

# *Are You Married?*

The man answered, yes, for 20 happy years,...while placing his deliveries into the company truck...

Do you believe in God? Of course, I do... Well, 04/19 is the birth of the earth...

You need to take your wife out on a date for the entire weekend...

I mean, really show her a good time... Buy her some shoes... No, these shoes, with stilettos and rhinestones...

I mean, get her a gold carpet gown...

Make sure you buy her 24kt gold that won't go off in the metal detectors... Get her hair styled by a Godly woman...

Make sure you sense her vibes... of evilness...

If you don't like how she is presented, then don't let her touch your wife's hair...because no filthy woman can put her demonic hands on your wife's sacred head. Now, when she walks in public, you walk behind her a bit and see what you have... However, grab her hand when people are staring too tough...and if she is respectful, she will never look into the welcoming eyes of sin...and yourself in vice versa... The man said I thank God for you... What's your name? It's nice to meet you... Thanks again, really... I needed that...

EXCUSES ME... Don't worry about the money... God will bless you...with more... However, you must show appreciation to your wife...or else...

God will make you pay…for taking advantage of your
blessings.

Make sure you take pictures as a memory… From only
God alone miracles…you will be in awe.

12:20p.m., on 04/18/2010.

## THE MINISTER WANTS A VIDEO...

I only have $500.00, but I want to work it off in another way… Now, I want to sell this video by the convention time…

I can make a lot of money…

My church secretary can work with you…but I saw your benefit package, and I can't afford to pay you even hourly…

Maybe we can make a deal…but it has to be only $500.00.

From this point on, God alone told the woman, no… Do not work with these people…

They denied you a chance to bring people into the church and deliver their souls

from evil…

However, when it came to their "church business…"

They wanted your support.

Don't ever do anything with them ever again in life…

This is my department, to deal with them…as only God alone chastises...

# "HEAVEN IS MY DOWRY AND FROM ONLY GOD ALONE THRONE."

A woman can request her husband to prove himself to only God alone as a Mu'men and have his soul heightened from only God-alone angels. This is more valuable than money…and vice versa; the husband can request for his wife to prove herself to only God alone in order to have both of their souls heightened and from only God alone.

Now, only God alone made us both pure in heavenly 24kt gold of 3.14 PI.

Now, if they don't want to be purified, then only God alone will have them replaced…and give you someone new…in their face.

It's a new day.

It is 8:20p.m., on July 05, 2011.

ANGELS CAN TEACH POTENTIAL
ANGELS IN TRAINING...

## *EVIL TWITCHES...*

Most people ride on energy with a swagger...

Even when they speak, in order to get their messages
across... Regardless, they still do it, and it sounds like
riddles...

Even if they're dead wrong...they fiddle with the truth...
While the illusions pretend not to know what to do...

Only the ignorant listen to crackhead decision makings and,
of course, from the negative side...

Without question,...ending their destinations at snafu rides
based on stinking

thinking...only in the demonic world...

This is how they get down in "coolness from their personal
gratification," with people that speak with a sun shade,
"cool," breeze kind of voice...

It's called the demonic...but yet sugar and sweet
voice...with illusions of the wind

and falsifying the message based on "energy."

It is 7:20a.m. on July 20, 2011

# *NEVER TURN THE WHEEL TO THE LEFT...AND AWAY FROM GOD...*

"When Satan's followers are involved…"

Please help me…

If I was willing…but I'm not… If my respect was not on the line…

If I was not in the way… If this, if that…

If my spouse…

If things were not tied up… If my friend would help…

Wait…time is of the essence… Work for only God alone is involved…

1 month goes by…

2 months goes by…

I don't know what you've told your spouse…but neither do I care… 3 months go by…

Please help me, somebody… Please…help me God alone…

Selfish speaks…God did tell me to help you…but either way…nothing bad doesn't happen…even if I don't…

Now the demonic follower bank account gets hijacked… Selfish speaks…God alone did tell me to help you… Sorry, I should've come to you first…

Woman to Woman…

And Or

Man to Man…

Whichever one who's really in need… Now we're in the 4th month… Now Satan is really involved…

Only God alone steps in…even more so…

God alone said, wait…selfishness is not going to cause the one in need to lose… Now, in order to teach the selfish a lesson…only God alone locks their money up…

# *NOW ONLY GOD ALONE EXTREMELY BEGINS TURNING THINGS AROUND...*

God alone says, listen here, selfishness… help the one in need right now… Or else…get killed and be burned in hell eternally at this very second…

The selfish speaks…

Here is your money…sorry…

God alone Angel lost nothing…because God alone saved it… It's called Never Mess with God Alone Angels…

The selfish get killed…for mockery…and using God's name in vain.

It is 8:19a.m., on July 20, 2011.

Never have friends that are willing to push you to the edge…

# *Talking To Satan's Followers...*

How do you iron your clothes without an iron?

Answering from Heaven?

You're going to hell… just come, wrinkled bitch… Oh my God…

No, you never included God alone in anything… You included… "Myself…"

Myself, Oh myself…

Oh, now "you are in hell…"

How about those out-cold believers that you were talking about… God doesn't need a gun…

God alone can fence on your soul... Even through a key hole with DEATH. It's hot…well, its hell…

Transition… It stings…

Well, it's freezing in hell… It's piercing…

Well, you pierced people with negative energy… You didn't think that you'd get it right back?

You caused hell… You lived hellish ways…

Now you will be in hellish times…
With infinity hellish rhymes…


"Now that's hot…"
It's 1:19p.m., on July 20, 2011.

# *HAIR DRESSER…*

Please style my hair… Hold on…

Can you keep a secret?

Well, okay, I'll trust you… My friend has a blood disease…

Please don't scratch her head too hard…because it might bleed… It's contagious…and I don't want anyone to

catch anything… Hairdresser, do you sanitize your tools before you use them? Well, if I have enough time, I will… Hairdresser, did you sanitize the tools that you are using on my head right now…? Can you keep a secret…no

ma'am, I was in a rush…? The doorbell rings…come on in… Hi Terry…this is the lady who just styled my hair… What…

Hairdresser, this is my friend Mary Ann…that I just told you about…

It is 8:20p.m., on July 20, 2011.

# *"Chicken And Biscuit Committee..."*

Wow, please come to our gathering… You will be treated like a Queen… Oh my God… What will she bring…?

Let's cook and share this hard-working celebration of the mid-year… Bring with you your 24kt. Gold hearts…of love…

Sacrificed will be appreciated while sharing 3.14PI, views of the International delight of fireworks…

What did she bring? Excuse me…

I want to help you… By the way, I bought you those chips, as well as the nuts…

Here you are, folks… Don't worry; here is something for the babies…

…I know that you've invited us to share…

But…my sister-in-law didn't care… She called you a hostess… Wow, your place is amazing… Let's run out quick before she notices…

Now slide the bags on the door knobs and pretend that some of the other guests ate…

By the way, here is your bottle of cheap wine…

We have a crew of 10…

Who wants to take fruit home…? The sister in law…said… ooh, me…

By the way…the wine spill will come up… We have to go now…

Don't worry about not cooking the raw hamburger…

We will take it home and cook it…even though we didn't bring anything cooked…

Can we see the boat race off of the river?

God said to me…

HELL NO…

Don't ever bring them back…

The kids are always welcome.

The others brought something delicious, and it's already cooked… It's more for everyone…

We will share equally… God is now pleased…

# *WHO GOES TO HELL?*

People that pierce others…

While forcing them into submission… Why God…

Why? LOL, God is God alone.

No one has the right to force others to do anything… Just today…a woman needed some help on her job…

The company Supervisor told her to lift heavy items…and her doctor restricted her due to back problems…

The woman was hurt, and the company refused to call the emergency units to assist her with

necessary medical attention…

Leaving the injured woman with no choice but to drive herself to the hospital… Later on, the company fired the injured employee…and denied her benefits…

Due to selfishness and as well as within the laws…

The selfish company blocked the injured woman from getting her lawsuit…stating in their argument that she violated the company's policy…and they won in the legal court system illegally… Now that same woman was elevated to the higher court…and she sued the company for the deed and won. The woman thanks only God alone for helping her overcome, and she helps others from a higher standpoint…but in submission to only God alone.

*MOVE YOURSELF OUT OF THE WAY AND FREELY OPEN YOUR HEART FOR ONLY GOD ALONE.*

## *SECURITY BREACH...*

Give the boss the percentage of increased and final sales each month… Make the boss happy…and if the boss wants more…do it…whatever it takes to stay ahead of the curve… Besides, this is our bread and butter; where else can we survive as the maintenance ungodly guy… Once we give the bosses what they want…that leaves the rest for us to keep… Now, this month, the big bosses want 85% of units rented…for the entire year… Listen up, crew…this leaves us 15% of what we want to do…in the fencing game… Now the economy is bad, so we have to do what is necessary to survive…even if we have to hire crack

heads…to make up the difference in our pockets by paying them very little and just enough to feed their

drug habits… Regardless, the tenants are required to get insurance…lol because it could be anybody stealing…even though we know the ends and outs of the building…. Nothing happens in our territory

without us knowing…we are the maintenance of ungodly people… Hey, boss… The guy's great job on the sales last month…

Now, I won't require 100% rental sales...because that's being greedy…

We are doing better than the surrounding apartments…and I don't want to lose any of you… Give yourselves a pat on the back…and pay increases are open for discussion before bonus season, and it will begin sooner than you think…

Now there is a riverfront apartment with 2 bedrooms and
1.5 baths

available for 1 full year, to the employee of the year… May
the best worker win…? Later guys… Later boss…

Now, 10% of the new tenants are complaining…and
threatening to move out… let's slow it down a bit…and
seem concerned…to keep them at least until half of the
year… Then we will start stealing again…just to keep the
police calls down… You know the boss checks those
complaints every other week… The last boss didn't
care…and we did what we wanted… Now, it's a little
different… I know because I have a family member who's
on the police force…and I have to pay him his cut for
information… in order to help us out and under the
table…through the organized crime fencing business.

# A Child's Morning Adventurer...

He's eight years old…with Jaguar capturing ideas…

Dad, please walk me to school today… I want to play with
my Jaguar… Son, your Jaguar? Yeah, that's what I call him
dad…

Son, but he lives in the forest…near the mountains…and
across the river… Yes, dad, I know…

So the son secretly brings his fighting belt…

Next thing the Jaguar meets the dad with his son…

The child remembers the relation that only God alone
showed him… The child began protecting his dad…with
swings evenly like sunrays… While balancing every hit…

All of a sudden, several boys come out and jump on the
eight-year-old boy…and his father grabs the
leather switch and began beating the boys away from his
son…as well as the Jaguar at the same time… Several men
who are friends of the son's father…saw the attacks and
came to defend them…while conquering it all…with only
strength from God alone…

The man said, thank God…

The man turned to his friend's and said, how can I repay
you?
They responded, God did

It is 3:14a.m., on July 21, 2011.

Two children about the ages of 5 and 7 years old… Were in the ocean swimming at sea… All of a sudden, an ocean whale comes by…and begins playing with them peacefully… Then the ocean demons began getting jcalous…and attempted to attack the boys…and God alone sent an Angel in disguise of a shark to attack the prey of the ocean world… Suddenly, the boys became free…and after God alone blew the water swish, swish, from side to side… While forcing a pathway to heaven, life, and freedom… Now the mother yells to the boys, "SONS, THANK ONLY GOD ALONE THAT YOU'RE OKAY… BECAUSE I CAN'T LIVE WITHOUT YOU…"

# GOD IS IN FULL CONTROL

Girls sing the blues…
Do whop… Girls sing it like a morning bird… That's how
God alone loves it…
The girls begin to sing again…and this time…
Angels fulfill their voice with music from God alone on the
throne.
Now the girls are hitting notes higher than the sky…and
heaven felt a heavenly vibe from earth… The crowd goes
wild…and hits a home run of peacefulness and joy…

God did it…the girls said…again… Thank God alone…

# *Please Help Me God Alone…*

People are coming by from the Mosque, and I don't have food today… God alone says yes, you do…

Take out those cans of string beans, chickpeas, and half a pound of hamburger…and don't forget the onion, with the ketchup and red vinegar cooking oil wine…

Now get your paprika, pepper, and garlic seasonings…as well as Italian… Let's get to work…

Wash those cans off…and get the can opener…and some olive oil… Now, Miss…the rest is up to you…

So the woman began seasoning the meat…and saying, please God, make it what you want…

The woman begins massaging the seasonings inside of the meat…, and then she adds the onions…

God alone said, hold on, now place the red wine cooking oil in the pan…and cook the string beans with your choice of flavors… One moment, cook the chickpeas separate…until both the string beans and chickpeas have their own flavor… Now cook the hamburger in a separate pan… Once all of the food is cooked… mix them together…but keep the chickpeas separate… Soak the chickpeas in a little red vinegar wine oil…and cook it slow… Now mix everything together…and you can add whatever seasonings that fulfill your soul… Now, Miss, grab the brown rice…and add Virginia extract olive oil… make sure that you rinse it out thoroughly, then fix the rice next…and then boil the water for pureness…

Now, make yourself some lemonade…and get you some pita bread from the refrigerator…and brown it just a little on the stove… My love, now it's a good time to get your plates… place a little gourmet filling that you've just cooked into the pita bread… add a little rice…and let it overflow onto the plate… Wait, darling, the cook always must taste the first serving… How do you like it…? Oh my

God…incredible… Now, quickly make the other plates… Is that the doorbell? Yes, it's your guest… Oh my God, we all followed the aroma to get to your apartment… We are ready for our gathering…and we brought some food to add to your dishes… Enjoy your homemade biscuits…from 33 years of experience because God alone told us to share 3.14PI, evenly like sunrays…

*REMEMBER, NEVER FORGET GOD.*

# *Help those whom only God alone tells you to help...*

Please help me…

I would help you, but…my man said no… My man doesn't like your man…

We'll God allowed me to help you spiritually, and you and your man are benefiting…

Do you mean to tell me that you are going to form a spiritual weapon against me…with the tools that God alone allowed me to show both of you… in order to become stronger in faith… Well, we do what God alone tells us to do…

God alone stopped them in their tracks…

Tell them…give them the money right now…

This is the very exact reason why people who worked so hard to follow me alone…fall apart due to your evil ways…

Some people go astray because they don't have any other foundation…after focusing on me alone,

God, the only God.

Do you know how this makes me look to the disbelievers, as well as the believers…?

Now you understand why you and your man…are destined to hell. Your man and you are not higher than me…the only God alone.

Go to hell with that stinking thinking…

Followers of God alone live well.

# *"GOD ALONE GIVES POINTS THAT PEOPLE FAIRLY EARNED TO MAKE IT INTO HEAVEN."*

This woman doesn't know that she is being tested for heaven and from only God alone. A woman meets another woman, and they become acquaintances… After several months…the woman in need's name is Bren Della, and the other woman's name is Quintintearritina, who can help financially. Bren Della says I'm having problems at my home…and the neighborhood is going downhill… Someone just tried to break into several homes on my block… Quincy, may I call you Quincy? Sure… Well, Quincy, can you help me out…with a top-of-the-line security system…I just noticed that my brand new car was stolen while we were on the phone… I just left from outside… How did they get past my alarm…? The company told me that it was secure… Now, what will I do? Bren Della, I feel for you…my family members told me about your street…but because she used to live around the corner from you…several years back… I would give you the money…but my husband doesn't like your family…and he said no. In my religion, you have to please your husband and God. Quincy, someone can come in on me…and no one will have proof… Yes, Bren Della, I know…what all of the factors are involved… Quincy, I can get killed…my next door neighbor did… Bren Della, I understand. I feel for you… Quincy, but not enough to help me secure my life…? I wouldn't say that… Bren Della. Quincy, yes, you are… Bren Della, I will not argue with you… Quincy says, excuse me, my husband just told me that he is taking me shopping…and he gave me $10,000.00; isn't that great. God is so good… Well, Bren Della, do you want to go window shopping with me? (God tells Bren Della to hang up the phone on Quincy)…

Bren Della was too nice…and kindly got off the phone…
Suddenly, Bren Della had to call the police over to her home…
Quincy said I couldn't sleep…so I got up and watched some
television…with a police chase scene involved… Bren Della said
last night I had to call the police…because someone walked in on
me in a ski mask…and that they cut my leg with a knife…and I
don't have enough money for the co-pay of surgery due to the
injuries… Quincy, please give me the money now… Bren Della, I
feel for you…God told me to help you…but either way, it doesn't
matter…my husband said no. I could die, Quincy. Yeah, I can't talk
to you anymore, Bren Della. I don't like people begging me for
anything, regardless… Now, it's 8 days before surgery…

(God alone makes Bren Della a pure 100% angel, who is no longer
human).

# *"GOD ALONE GIVES POINTS THAT PEOPLE FAIRLY EARNED TO MAKE IT INTO HEAVEN."*

Bren Della gets her house fired bomb with her husband in it… Now God approaches them and says you can't please me and the devil… Your husband is the son-in-law of the devil… Didn't you notice the evil negative energy in the situation Quintintearritina? God, I'm confused… Confused about what, Quintintearritina? Using your heart is the key to getting into heaven… Obviously, you and your husband don't have any heart…and in heaven, you need a pure 24kt gold heart to float 3.14 PI.

Don't worry. Hell is your home…and it lives with deadweight. (God alone calls Bren Della…)

God tells Bren Della, I saved your soul before the criminals came into your home… This is why you never felt anything… My darling, you still have the memory that I uploaded into your brain…but you were safe on earth the entire time… Bren Della, Quintintearritina, and her husband never had any family…here are the deeds to her vacation homes, cars…as well as information to her bank accounts… Don't worry, and an angel from heaven will be waiting for you at the banks…as well as inside the Attorney's offices… Bren Della never wondered about anything else…from here on out.

Bren Della says, answers yes, God alone has the honors, and throws both of the demonic bitches into the piercing point of hell… Quincy yells, "BREN DELLA, NO… ALL WHAT I DID FOR YOU…" Bye handkerchief heads…

Thank you only God alone.

# *NEVER COME EMPTY HANDED...TO A DINNER...*

You're invited...

What should I bring?

Nothing, all of the food is already prepared...just bring yourself...

Are you sure?

Yes, it's my friend's house, and she is cooking Thanksgiving dinner... Okay, then, here I come...

The doorbell rings...

Who are you?

Cynthia...

We don't know Cynthia...

Is Julia in...? Wait right there... Yeah, she said, come around to the side door... Hi everyone... No one speaks...everyone has a look on their faces...

"Who is this?" Julia invited me... Julia, well, come on in... The television is in the guest room...

After 30 minutes, someone says...

Do you want something to eat?

No, thank you... I think I will leave now... Wait, it is okay if you eat first... Okay... Thank you... Take a plate home. It is okay... Thank you, it's nice meeting everyone...

# *Hi, Welcome to the Plaza...*

Where we aim to please your height of the living riverfront standards… Meet your maintenance workers…anything that you need, just ask them…

By the way, enjoy your new home…and before you go, please place your bags…inside the apartment…and let's go downstairs and speak….

One moment, please… Manager… my phone is ringing… Lettyia, is that you? Yes, Attorney John… Lettyia, don't leave your bag inside the apartment unless you are certainly sure that you will live there… Why do you say that, Attorney John…? Well, the moment that you leave anything inside of the rental unit, you have legally taken possession of the apartment… This is a legal tactic that these apartment and or rental people take…as finalizing their contractual agreement… Thank you, Attorney John… One more thing, Lettyia, if anyone that's administering the contractual signing splits the contract up during their presentation, watch out because they have something that's very serious that's happening inside of their property, and it is illegal, and they don't want to invest in the money in order to stop the crime… Manager, no thank you, but I won't need this apartment at this time… I have to go attend to a sick family member down south… I just got the call; please keep me on file… Certainly Ms. Lettyia…I appreciate your candor.

# *WHEN DEMONS...SCREW UP...*

God just has them pick up a gun and or weapon and kill themselves… for demonic behavior… This is God alone's best work…

Having the demons destroy themselves…

God is so good…and cleans up the earth with the "garbage thinkers…"

One time, a demon placed his gun on the table facing him… and God allowed the death angels to pull

the trigger…shooting him…

It was amazing no one else was around…

The police had no choice but to close the case… God moves in mysterious ways…

Be careful out there…

God alone takes to heart…how everyone treats only God alone people.

There is no such thing as a leader other than only God alone...but there is such a thing as followers of only God alone.

Jennifer Thomas, 3.14 Pl name is Mu'men 'Elleyyeen.

All of God alone materials charge the messages for the mind only... Although nothing that's tangible is for sale... just the message only...

Only God alone gets all of the credit.

Only God alone is the leader.

# *Little People at Your Service...*

Good day; how can we help you?

Well, we have a little problem at home…and we need to catch a fencer in the act…

One moment, sir, what is your name?

Jerry Lee, that is Jerry Lee with two r's…

Okay, thanks, sir. What would you like us to call you?

Larry is fine… Okay, thank you, Larry…

Please let us ask you a few questions… Certainly…

How long has this fencing problem been going on?

Oh, about the last seven months… Okay, you need us immediately…?

Yes, I do?

Well, Larry, it is our job to study the demographics in the area…

What is your zip code?

48214.

Okay then, you reside in a well-rounded economic status…

# *LITTLE PEOPLE AT YOUR SERVICE...*

I would say that...

Okay, Larry, we have the right plan for you...

Please meet us near Belle Isle with a rolling suitcase bag...in the nearby restaurant in the men's bathroom...

Excuse me; is this some kind of joke, sir?

No sir...

You did call little people at your service for a fencing problem, right?

Yeah...

Well, here is a little person for you... His name is Harry...

Harry is flexible and can operate in any condition...

Harry has caught people in the white collard government-secured areas... So he can catch even a hood rat cheating on her man...

By the way, we have that service for you for only $599.00 for a discounted price... Typically, when we work in the "hood," it may be a little gang banging...

So we make our people gang-banging ready...

Now, where exactly do you stay, sir...?

# *LITTLE PEOPLE AT YOUR SERVICE...*

On Jefferson... What within 9000 block? Yes, how did you know?

We get a lot of calls from that area...

You know Larry, for example; it reminds me of a "crackheadasonian..." Why do you say this...?

Well, when a crackhead wants a job, he and or she cleans them up...at least until they get inside...those riverfront places...and then all of a sudden, police are being called... Lookouts are thugs, drunks...as well as the local gang bangers...even hill Billie's work in this area...

Do you know bikers?

Oh yeah...

Larry, we got you covered...

From now on, don't leave anything important in your rental unit...

# LITTLE PEOPLE AT YOUR SERVICE...

Larry, we will cut you a discount and only charge you $1,000 dollars.

Wow, and in the hood, is it $599?

Well, Larry, that's an advertised secured area…and things are a bit different… You have what you call an inside job…preferably on every floor…

Besides, we have a monthly drawing to our first-time customers…of $1,000,000,000. Get me out of here… God alone is your emergency exit kind of day…

Oh wow, and I do need God alone.

Perfect, Larry, we may pay for this service ourselves, depending on how things go…

Will I still be able to get involved in the raffle?

Of course, Larry, God is good all the time.

You know, Larry, God does not bless people on contingency status.

Thank God

Please, someone, answer the phone…

# *Little People At Your Service…*

Hi, my name is Qarry Young, and I'm looking for an available job position…

Uh, Qarry Young, how did you hear about us?

My brother Derrick he used to work for you guys…about 10 years ago… Oh yes, Derrick…how is he doing?

Derrick is doing fine…

Good to hear. Tell him Rick says hi… I sure will…

Now, Qarry, are you a great worker like your brother?

Okay, we will perform a thorough background check…" Military-style…" Let me ask you, Qarry, is everything okay before we begin this process…?

As far as I know, sure… Okay then…

Now you do know the requirements, right?

Well, if it's still the same as when my brother was working at your company, yeah…

You have to be about 2ft, between 50 and 75 lbs.

That's great, Qarry; now add to that in great health…very fast, and in shape…

Now, Qarry, we do have a doctor on board because sometimes people don't follow their diet.

# *LITTLE PEOPLE AT YOUR SERVICE...*

Qarry, before we hire you, we need to know that you will follow this strict, healthy diet that will even

help a heart attack victim recover…

What we mean by this is… Qarry you will have to jump out of bags very fast…

Well, we will send you through a training process…to help you move along before you begin work… Now we have a monkey on board…and he is already trained…

A monkey, did you say monkey?

Why yes, Qarry, we measure our speed with nature best in this field…

God showed us one day when we went to the zoo… me and my brother Furry was having hard time rubbing pennies together…

I mean, that monkey was swinging tree to tree, rope to rope… Qarry, that's the explanation behind our logo, by the way…

Qarry, the monkey's name, is Ben, and we have provided a video for you to communicate with the monkey…in order for you to understand its commands…

Qarry, I know how this sounds…but keep in mind, in training, you get paid $50.00 per hour.

After the training period, you get paid $100.00 per hour.

Now, Qarry, we have to do these things to keep people safe inside of their homes…

The reason being, my cousin's mother got robbed, and no one could catch the guy…because he was so fast,

and he even had a lookout welcoming committee for an entourage…

# *LITTLE PEOPLE AT YOUR SERVICE...*

Qarry, we have captured millions since the first day that we opened... We can't wait to get you trained...

Qarry, are you busy now?

No sir...

Okay, my brother Furry will pick you up to get this process started...

Now, before you do, are you okay with wearing a ski mask?

A ski mask?

Yes, Qarry, we can't have the criminals learning your face...

Besides, we want our people to relax when they're in the public eye... Okay, well, we will provide all of the equipment for you, with no problem...

Qarry, once again, it's good to hear that Derrick is your brother, and just so you know, our senior worker

is 90 years old.

Did you say 90 years old?

Yes, we don't discriminate; he can do the job better than the monkey... Hey darling, God is amazing...

The more the merrier...okay...

Now, Qarry, if you were to describe yourself, what animal and/or bird would you compare yourself to as far as the jungle world goes?

Well, Rick, I would have to say a Jaguar.

A Jaguar, oh wow…

Okay, I don't believe we have one of those…

Now, Qarry, if everything checks out, just because of your energy status, you will get paid $4,000 per week.

Qarry, you are rare, and we recognize your talents…

Yeah, Qarry, God teaches us that our worker's labor is worth their pay… Qarry, if everything checks out, and you're what you weigh…

Hey, one moment, my brother says that you guys pay very well…yes, even more so today…

Qarry, if your brother Derrick wants to come back, tell him that we will take very good care of him…

We have a new store opening up privately, of course, in the Detroit, Michigan area… Tell him to name his price, and we will gladly pay him…whatever it is… trust me… Tell him to include the best style of living package, and it will most definitely be on the table for him as a done deal…

(Qarry chuckles, money laughs…)

Of course, Rick, I sure will… I will call him right now…

# *Little People At Your Service...*

Qarry, if your brother Rick comes back, we will offer you a bonus pay… it's…called employee returning

referral bonus package… When this happens, we will tell you at the time… It's more than awesome… Qarry, God approved it in my revelation…

Qarry we pay very well, and we respect our people to the fullest…with no limitations… Qarry, God is…

I will finish that, Rick… Good, all the time… Say it again Qarry…

"God is good all the time."

Hey Qarry, by the way, we have a personal trailer, so you don't need to meet us in a nearby restaurant.

Restroom okay?

God alone upgraded our business earlier this year… All praises be to God alone…

Qarry we would like you to build a personal relationship with Ben…

Who is Ben?

Oh the monkey… That's correct Qarry…

Now, he likes long walks on the beach...near Belle Isle...

There's this other monkey that visits there as well pretty often...

Now, be careful not to let him do his monkey business...because some days the both of you will be on call, okay...

Yeah Okay, Rick...

Alright Qarry, that's enough for right now...

Wait, Rick, is there more...yeah but right now, we want you to focus on what is in front of you...

Qarry, have a great first day... Bye, Rick... Later.

ANY OF THE MATERIAL, AS WELL AS
IDEAS THAT ARE
WITNESSED...BELONGS TO ONLY GOD
ALONE... TO ME, AS THE CHOSEN
ONE; AND NO ONE ELSE; UNLESS ONLY
GOD ALONE TELLS ME TO GIVE IT TO
YOU PERSONALLY...

# "GOD, PLEASE HELP ME STUDY…"

My children keep fighting through arguments…

Sure, my dear,

Whisper your homework to each of your children…

Now, dear, give them their favorite fruit while you read
your homework in front of them… Play with their
hair…and massage their scalps…

Now, dear, keep doing this for several days…

After one week, they will read your homework back to you,
by memory…and help you pass your exams…in order for
you to pay your bills and take them out for fun…

By the way, dear, give them a fun day experience, and each
time you get paid, give them something

affordable, and based on your budget in return…

At this time, they will want more, and they will cooperate
without chastising's… Thank you only God alone.

# *"DON'T GIVE UP..."*

This is your home; it came from God alone. Stand your ground…force the fencers to leave… The fencers are stuck, not you…

God gave us education, jobs, and so forth… This is our heavenly life as well as freedom…

The fencers are the rats, so chase them out of your house… DON'T YOU RUN ANYMORE…

Hell awaits them…just trust only God alone.

If you don't know how to stand up; then pray to only God alone for a lesson… God will show you in a way that you will understand…

For example, chase the rat towards the door, and scare the rodent…it will run out for freedom…

It's called the trap that you set for me you will fall in it yourself…

Thank you only God alone.

From months after the illegal entries were discovered within The Jeffersonian Apartments, it became very difficult to recover finances…from all of the extremely hard work that it took to move into the building… Even after several months of legally chasing the police for help, my funds were running low because my workload was back-dated from the evilness within The Jeffersonian building… That's when I had no choice but to live off of my savings…as well as my collector's coin items…and all the way up to 07/22/2011…with a $300.00 loan. The reason being, several years back, when Allah had me working, God told me to put away food, as well as extra money to survive during hard times…and I listened… It's amazing how God worked things out… Even when the neighbors upstairs cut holes in the floors and entered my apartment, with the inside workers…tapping into my electricity…and raising my energy bills to shut-off status without me knowing… I paid the bills, and all I have even plugged up today is a small clock radio and refrigerator, as well as one electric stove… Furthermore, I save energy quite often…and it saves resources… Moreover, going back into time, on June 08, 2011, I got a shutoff notice, and I 'm glad that I listened to God not to open either of my television boxes…because I needed to pawn them both for money…due to lack of funds regarding the Jeffersonian Apartments insiders… and fencing business that set my life backward… Moreover, even during the weekend just before the fireworks on June 26, 27, 28, 29…and so forth in 2011, I couldn't get anyone to help me financially… I even applied to Walden University to start classes the week of

June 27, 2011…and when I asked the instructor for understanding of misprinted information…she briefly described, but not enough to clarify the results…which led to a bigger problem… So I saw a phone number to contact her on-line…and the instructor did not return the phone call… The next thing happened: I called my advisor and asked my advisor to switch classes because I needed a welcoming instructor with concern… Furthermore, as a result, Walden University kicked me out of the program and told me because of no activity, I couldn't attend any course…regardless… At this time, I couldn't believe it because this educational institution could have helped to bridge my financial resources and would have helped me gracefully… The reason being that the School of The Art Institute of Chicago held back consolidation balances…that prevented me from attending any other school…as a result of a legal protest to provide me my student disabilities…in order to have a 3.14PI blissful recovery… That a former roommate harassed me repeatedly back in the year of 2008, with the support of The School of The Art Institute of Chicago and …by way of aggravating my injuries…as well as causing more injuries….

# *STRUGGLING...*

The School of The Art Institute of Chicago even stole medical information that led to Dr. Sew in Southfield, Michigan, at the time... Dr. Sew's medical office gave out medical information that did not regard the present injury at hand...as well as appears to be in cohoused with The Michigan Avenue Immediate care with Dr. Kary, located in Chicago, IL. Dr. Kary harassed me into giving her information after she heavily prescribed medication for medical treatment...and she kept repeating the same question after I said no to her giving any information as well as communication with The School of The Art Institute of Chicago. I was just about to pass out, and she knew when to call because she gave me the dates and times when to take my medication until it was gone... Furthermore, this misinformation that was sent behind my back, and without my consent, was not updated, and they did not see me regarding the disability with the Toyota Camry vehicle break failures, as well as the steering wheel malfunctioning...that caused me to go about 15ft in the air and landed abruptly...with a prayer to only God alone for saving my life... The car could've swung off of the overpass, into the river...and also into several mac trucks... Moreover, the insurance company AAA never came...due to back-ups. I called back, and the representative said that they did not have my name in the system... At this time the sheriff of New Baltimore assisted me... Anyhow, these are setbacks, and they will be discussed later on... it's truly my real-life experiences...

*STRUGGLING...*

*Positive is at the top, &*

*Negative is at the bottom.*

# "ADVENTURERS WITH ONLY GOD ALONE"

Everyone is in the living room with cathedral ceilings…loft style… All of a sudden, the walls began to tumble with earth-quaking sounds… Afterward, we all noticed that nothing had moved out of place…not even one inch. Then my friend Adam came by from the bible days, and he rescued me from the crowd of fear… We ran upstairs and down a steep hill, that's attached to the home… We climbed ropes that were

tied up for miles… Adam is so amazingly in shape…his mind is magnificent…and of course, from only God alone. I couldn't believe that I was having this experience…with a great guy and from only God alone.

Adam showed me how to survive in the mountains, as well as in the woods, for 40 days and 40 nights. Adam told me that God sent him to me for protection… Adam's mind is so clever, and when it comes to fighting war… he was great at playing chess.

During our adventurer and from only God alone, we passed this young boy, that's a superstar in his time… That's when I found some black and green shoes with a mix of nature's gold… I didn't have my pocket book on me, so I asked him if he had mine…and the boy said okay, you hold it…

# "ADVENTURERS WITH ONLY GOD ALONE"

I told him, you know how things are…people play the race card all of the time… The young boy said okay, but I don't want to, but then okay…why not… The young boy said wait here…have some food. My party is at 4p.m., and we are serving pork on pizza… I told him I couldn't do the pork thing… He said to have some chili and cheese fries…

I said sure, thank you very much… After eating, Adam and I became close friends…and only from God alone. I told Adam that he is the coolest guy…and how wonderful God alone made him… People need to focus on the inner…to meet their soul.

Oh, we should never have entered her place… Man, I thought you said that she

signed over her rights… She did; we saw her…

You mean, you thought you did… Okay, well now we all have to pay her bills evenly like sunrays… You mean we have to pay the tenant's rent?

Yeah, if we don't, she could sue the big boss, and we will lose our jobs…

How can we do that since we filed court papers on her and illegally? Well, sometimes we have to withdraw our complaint and pay off the judge to keep the judge from telling the big bosses what happened… So, you mean to tell me that we have to give the tenant a portion of our pay checks? Pretty much… and you illegally entered her unit without her permission and vandalized her expensive things… Well, she was mean to me… Well, it's your own fought. You illegally entered her home without her permission…set down on her brand-new furniture, ate her fruit, and cost her money… We should have a get-together and jump on you "313 style…"

Okay, your point is taken, sorry…

# *"Barbers Get Paid Good…"*

Charlie, I can't believe that I let you guys talk me out of being a barber…

I mean business men come into the shops all of the time, talking about how to make more money… Several of my family members benefited from their ideas… Well, Jim, did they pay them some gratitude cash? No… This is what I mean about users… Charlie, how is that a user? Well, they didn't have to tell several of your

relatives anything… Besides, their wealth of ideas comes from the struggles off of their backs and rewards from only God alone. Tell me, Jim, where do you fit into all of their blessings? Exactly… someone sounds like a loser to me… Come on Shawn, I think we're done here… Charlie, your phone is ringing… LOL, broke sounds… Anyway, hi who's calling? It's Sherry you know that apartment that you need? Yeah, well, there is a unit opened in my building…don't worry about the paperwork; just make out a check and move yourself into it right away… I heard that the owners are having trouble with their marketing company, and they need you… It's a surprise… Really are you sure? Jim, who will turn down money these days? Okay, I guess you're right…

Barbershop Jim, did you hear that Charlie listened to Sherry and the owners dialed 911…?

Tell Jim Willy to meet me outside… What's the reason behind your story this time…?

Well, I need him to follow me to his truck with his head lights on, so I can see at

night… What?

That's ridiculous… Canita, hear me out…

Well, I'm riding my big wheel tonight because someone let the air out of my tires…

Cindy, don't you have an air pump…?

It's at the gas station…

Do you guys hear this…no wonder the judge took custody of your children…?

You're mean, Catina…

No I'm not, honey you told the judge that rats are your pets… Get help already…

I told you how to pray to only God alone, but you still choose to idol worship… No one can help you…

# 

I'm not scared… Take me to the jungle…

I want to live like the Africans lived during Kente's days…

Excuse me, do you speak the language?

I got a monkey at home… Is this a prank call?

No, I'm serious… How much is my trip going to cost me?

What do you mean…other than money?

Well, let me guess: common sense is not one of them… I can tell… I resent this… my dad is a lawyer…

Whoops, you shouldn't tell anyone that information… They may not let you come to Africa guerrilla style… One moment, what's your name: Juwangi Monkey… Really? That's my name…

Boy, it gets better… Okay, Juwangi, come in and pick up your boarding pass today…

Thank you, sir… Hey, bring $1,000.00. No problem sir.

# Minimum Wage...

Day after day, scrub the floors the toilets...and sweep as well as mop the floors... All we get paid is $5.55 per hour, while the "big bosses" get the big paychecks off of our hard-working backs... Where is our 3.14PI, and from only God alone. I feel like every day that we come to work without benefits, we are getting robbed...and why? The reason being, because of a bad economy, that can't be proven even with "The Supreme Being Life Cycle Equation" system, as an excuse, day after, day after day... When does it end...I need to feed my children just like everyone

else... ...Then several of the people died from cancer here at this company due to inhaling fumes from cleaning after 25 years... This year in 1997, if they give me another crack head pay, I'm going to do a crack head job...as a protest for my rights and from only God alone.

# *Mommy, I don't like him...*

Shut up, girl, he is going to be your dad regardless of what you say… Mommy, but he is not a good person… Yes, he is. He brings me money to pay all of the bills… Mommy but dad called yesterday and said that he is coming with a check for

$50,000 to finish paying off the house note so that we don't have to worry about anything… Really, $50,000.00…yes mommy really… Okay, this man isn't worth losing $50,000.00. Let me call this wedding off…right now… Hi Bill, um, things are not working out between us anymore. My children need their dad…

Carolyn, what do you mean we are not working out anymore… Aren't you happy with me? You're a really great guy, but I have to do what's best for my children… Okay, as you wish… Take good care, and if you want to talk sometime, give me a call…my phone number is still the same… Okay Bill, take good care… You to

Carolyn… When everyone fell asleep, Carolyn's baby girl Sheba, who's 5 years old, was in a revelation that her mother Carolyn witnessed… Only God alone made Sheba extremely strong in her foundation…and she swung on top of her mother's

house swinging it left to right…as the wind blew…she swung even harder… Carolyn looked outside of her house, and she couldn't believe how strong that only God alone made her daughter… So the very next day, Carolyn heard

Sheba saying again, Mommy, I don't like that man, and this time she listened…

Sheba, thank you only God alone.

# *BABY GETS CHILD ABUSER BACK...*

The child abuser slapped the baby 1 time in the face...and it cried continuously...but no one heard... So the child abuser fell asleep, and God made the baby strong, and the Angles picked up the baby, and the baby kicked the child abuser in the face 40 times until she died... Then the Angels put the baby back into the baby's crib and took the baby to heaven to wipe away the pain...and brought the baby back when the mother was opening up her front door... "OH MY GOD THE MOTHER YELLED..." What happened, and the child abuser babysitter was dead... Then the baby rolled over and went to sleep...as if nothing happened...

## DON'T PUT YOUR BABY ANYWHERE, AND WITH ANYONE...

This man and woman had a baby out of wedlock…and they always let anyone watch their baby… At the baby's birth, the doctor told them not to put important numbers in front of the baby's face…because he will remember them and use them later… Well, these parents didn't listen…and they let a family member who was a bank robber watch their baby… Well, the baby remembers the bank codes…and when he got older, the police matched the baby to the crime… 20 years later, by its hair… The court called the now-grown baby to trial…and his attorney reported to the court that it was ridiculous; he was only a baby… The courts reported, yeah, but look at his record now…trouble didn't fall too far from the baby's crib… Your

…Honor, but, but… Excuse me, Mr. Attorney, your client left gold blondish hair 20 years ago…and again 20 years later, the same exact hair shows up again at the same bank… What are the odds of this…? LOL… uh Judge, his uncle brought him with them to rob the bank when he was a baby… LOL, Mr. Attorney, does it make it right…? This is a hard question, considering all of the facts… Mr. Attorney, we are ready to sentence your client up to 25 years in prison as the second offense… Mr. Attorney, this sentence will prevent the next family generation from robbing another bank…let this be a lesson learned.

# "ANOTHER CLOUD IS OVER THE CITY OF DETROIT…"

Everyone is screaming, while only God alone sends the whispers of the wind…pressuring even the car alarms to sing… As the sky becomes dim and the clouds form into darkness…people start to run…and say, "Hell is coming on earth…" God alone laughs and flushes the city with rain and pushes the waves within the water, from side to side…all the way under, and even passing the Belle Isle Bridge… Children are running as well as screaming… God alone whispers in their ears, relax, this fear isn't for you, and it's for your disobedient parents… As the streets become slippery, the cars are forced to slow down…and the sky rides with energy… while sending a communication to the fog, to whiten the vision from way under to high above… Wherever you are, stay put, and let the chastising continue…I told you that only God alone is on the menu…

# CITY OF SILHOUETTE

Have you ever seen a silhouetted city? When it rains, the wind darkens, and only God alone takes the sun on a shaded ride… While sending the wind through the clouds and surrounding as darkness… The next thing you hear is God alone stomping thunder from heaven and becoming angry at the sinners who just don't care about being righteous… Sometimes, during the silhouette storm, many of them don't make it home…

# *SOUNDS OF THE STORM...*

Have you ever paid attention to the sounds of the storm?

It sounds like airplanes landing...after a long fight...

From hours after take-off, nature repeats itself over and over again...

Until we all get the message from only God alone throne. The message says, move when only God alone says to move... It's called follow only God alone.

It's 7:20p.m., on July 24, 2011.

# ANGELS FORM WITHIN THE CLOUDS...

The angel is forming into a newborn baby… inside of its mother's womb… Birthing itself through funnel shapes of raptures and transforming as one huge cloud…

Now it's moving into full force, from The Ambassador Bridge, back and forth into slow movement… All the way from Canada to the U.S.A. while landing here in Detroit, Michigan. While the clouds bring a story, and from only God alone, it

says, "get it together, or else… the next time; poof… gone with the wind…"

*Remember, this story is only the beginning of the end.*

*GOD IS IN FULL CONTROL*

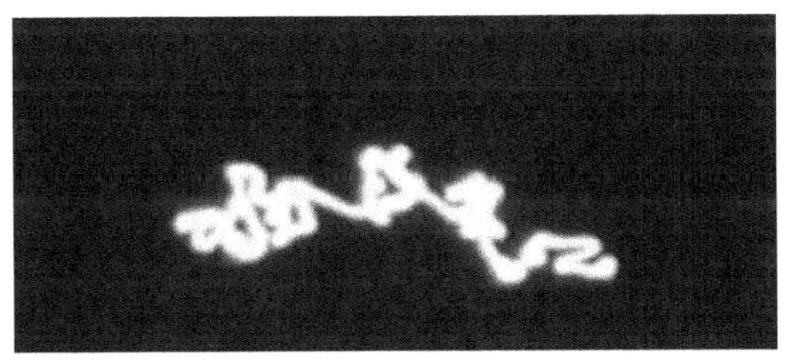

**BY Jennifer DiAnne Thomas**

**Time Is In Reverse Part II**

**Copyright © 2011**